BUG TEAM ALPHA

JUGGERNAUT

Laurie S. Sutton
illustrated by Patricio Clarey

Raintree is an imprint of Capstone Global Library Limited,
a company incorporated in England and Wales having its
registered office at 264 Banbury Road, Oxford, OX2 7DY –
Registered company number: 6695582

www.raintree.co.uk
myorders@raintree.co.uk

Designer: Hilary Wacholz

Printed and bound in India.

ISBN 978-1-4747-5462-0
22 21 20 19 18
10 9 8 7 6 5 4 3 2 1

British Library Cataloguing in Publication Data
A full catalogue record for this book is available from
the British Library.

...n to reproduce
...roughout
...n elements:

...lders of
...ill be rectified
...blisher.

CONTENTS

Bug Team Alpha is the most elite special operations force of the Colonial Armed Forces of the Earth Colonial Coalition. Each member has an insect's DNA surgically grafted onto his or her human DNA. With special abilities and buglike features, these soldiers are trained to tackle the most dangerous and unique combat missions. Their home base is Space Station Prime.

Ariel "Dragonfly" Carter

A human female with dragonfly wings grafted onto her shoulder blades. She is slender and lightweight, always on her tiptoes and ready for flight.

Rank: Commander
Age: 30 Earth Years
Place of Origin: Earth,
    European Hemisphere
Hair: Blonde
Eyes: Blue
Height: 1.8 metres

Gustav "Burrow" Von Braun

A human male with digger beetle arms grafted onto his torso. He is heavyset and very strong and muscular.

Rank: Lieutenant
Age: 24 Earth Years
Place of Origin: Earth,
    European Hemisphere
Hair: Brown
Eyes: Brown
Height: 1.58 metres

Irene "Impact" Mallory

A human female with a beetle exoskeleton grafted onto her body. She's always slightly hunched over like a wrestler ready to tackle an opponent.

Rank: Lieutenant
Age: 24 Earth Years
Place of Origin: Earth, European Hemisphere
Hair: Red
Eyes: Brown
Height: 1.68 metres

Sancho "Locust" Castillo

A human male with bug wings and carapace grafted onto his back. He has immense strength and flying capabilities.

Rank: Lieutenant
Age: 23 Earth Years
Place of Origin: Earth, South American Hemisphere
Hair: Light brown
Eyes: Brown
Height: 1.83 metres

Akiko "Radar" Murasaki

A human female with cranial antennae grafted onto her forehead. She can sense vibrations and determine the distance between and shape of objects in dark spaces.

Rank: Lieutenant
Age: 28 Earth Years
Place of Origin: Earth, Asian Hemisphere
Hair: Black
Eyes: Brown
Height: 1.58 metres

Madhuri "Scorpion" Singh

A human female with scorpion stingers grafted onto her hands. She can knock out an enemy with the venom.

Rank: Lieutenant
Age: 24 Earth Years
Place of Origin: Earth Colony Shiva Three
Hair: Black
Eyes: Brown
Height: 1.8 metres

CHAPTER 1

Lieutenant Gustav "Burrow" Von Braun of Bug Team Alpha stood on the bridge of the *Resolve*, a Colonial Armed Forces destroyer-class spacecraft. The ship was nearing the orbit of Pluto, and a gigantic asteroid filled the monitor screen. Burrow studied the image and crossed all four of his heavily spiked arms.

Captain Addo stood next to the lieutenant, but not too close. The captain had a muscular build almost as impressive as Burrow's massive bug-DNA-enhanced body. But those spikes were intimidating.

"That asteroid doesn't look so special," Burrow muttered. "Except that it's really, really big."

"And on a collision course with Earth," Captain Addo reminded him. "Which is why we're here to destroy it."

"That should be a simple task with the *Resolve*'s firepower," Burrow said.

"It might take a few rounds of plasma torpedoes," the captain admitted. "After all, that asteroid is over fifty kilometres wide. Still, it's nothing the *Resolve* can't handle."

Burrow watched the monitor. The huge rock was tumbling through space towards Earth's solar system. Burrow briefly wondered where in deep space the asteroid had come from. More importantly, however, he knew for certain where it was headed.

"There are a couple of things to do before we reduce it to rubble," Burrow noted. "The tech department wants me to try out some prototype space armour on the asteroid's surface. Although I don't know why we needed to come all the way out here to test it."

Captain Addo shrugged. He didn't know either. However, it didn't interfere with his primary mission to destroy the asteroid threatening Earth. So the captain was willing to indulge a team of techs from the Research and Development Department.

"From what I understand, the armour was designed just for you," the captain said.

"Yes, sir. It's supposed to allow me to use my digging spikes in the vacuum of space and other hostile environments," Burrow replied. He flexed his arm spikes. The captain instinctively stepped back.

"Well, the surface of that asteroid is as hostile as it gets. Good luck," Captain Addo said, and saluted Burrow.

"Yes, sir. Thank you, sir," Burrow replied, returning the salute. Knowing that he had been dismissed, he turned and left the bridge.

One Earth Standard hour later, Burrow set foot on the asteroid's surface, wearing the experimental armour. He practically bounced across the moon-like terrain of dusty soil and small rocks. The asteroid had a weak gravitational field, which made the heavy armour feel as light as a feather.

A small observation drone floated alongside him. The R&D tech team had stayed aboard the *Resolve* and were using the drone to watch the armour test.

The drone pointed a strong spotlight at Burrow to illuminate him in the sunless night of space.

Burrow began the test. He quickly dug about a metre down into the soil. "This is easy," he reported.

"Good. It's supposed to be," one of the R&D techs said over the comm. "Now, we need to test how the prototype armour holds up over longer use. Let's try digging a trench for about a hundred metres."

Burrow completed the task with no problems. The only hard part was keeping himself from flying off the asteroid's surface in the weak gravity.

"I'm not even out of breath," Burrow told the techs. "I need something more challenging. I'm going to see how deep I can go."

Before the tech team could argue, Burrow started digging deep. He used his bug-DNA-enhanced strength to churn his armoured spikes through layers of dirt and rock. He did not get far.

THUNK! The armoured spikes hit something hard.

"What's this?" Burrow exclaimed.

He quickly removed a patch of soil. The observation drone hovered overhead, trying to get a clear view as

Burrow tossed up clouds of asteroid dust. At last, he uncovered a layer of solid metal.

"Is that … a ship's hull?" one of the techs asked.

"Looks like it to me," Burrow replied, tapping it with his armoured knuckles. "A ship must have crashed and got buried. Hard to say how long it's been here."

"Burrow, why don't you excavate it? It'll be a good test of the armour," a tech suggested.

So Burrow began to dig. And dig. And dig. After nearly an Earth Standard hour of excavation, Burrow had cleared a square kilometre of the asteroid's surface. He still could not find where the ship's hull ended. All he found were small hatches. That confirmed there was definitely a vessel of some sort under the soil.

Burrow stood at the edge of his handiwork. He looked out over the wide metal surface. It gleamed like polished copper, even in the permanent midnight of space.

"This can mean only one of two things," Burrow told the techs over the comm. "Either this buried spaceship is really big, or this is no asteroid."

"You think that the asteroid is a *spaceship*?" General Barrett asked in astonishment as he spoke with Burrow and Captain Addo via video comm.

General Barrett was commanding officer of the Colonial Armed Forces. He was sitting in his office on Space Station Prime in orbit above Earth. The general ran a hand over his bald head. It was a gesture he often made when he was agitated.

This new information changed the *Resolve*'s mission parameters. And the information continued to get more and more incredible as Burrow and Addo gave their report.

"That's correct, sir. The *Resolve* has made a complete sensor sweep of the asteroid – I mean, the spacecraft," Captain Addo said. "The hull is made from an unknown metal alloy, but it's been covered with a thick layer of space dust. Our sensors can't get through the hull, but we've mapped the surface terrain. I'm transmitting images now."

As Barrett watched the images scroll by, Addo continued. "There's a row of low mountains on one side of the asteroid. They look naturally formed, but we believe they're actually the exhaust ports of some kind of propulsion system. There's no energy residue that we can detect. So we don't know what sort of energy is used for propulsion, and we can't tell when the system was last fired," Captain Addo said.

"Have we been able to communicate with the ship?" Barrett asked.

"No, sir," Addo responded. "We've tried all standard protocols."

"It might be a relic, sir," Burrow suggested. He almost sounded excited. "Some piece of ancient alien technology, abandoned and drifting through space. In any case, the tech needed to build a ship that size must be very advanced."

"Yes, it might be a relic, and it may have advanced technology," the general agreed. "But that thing is still on a collision course with Earth. And that makes it a problem."

"Sir, I request permission to go aboard," Burrow said. "This could be a valuable research opportunity – too valuable to simply destroy it. I may be able to find the bridge and stop the ship from hitting Earth. Then we could bring it in for study. If that fails, the *Resolve* can blow it up as planned."

General Barrett considered Burrow's request. The asteroid ship was still outside the orbit of Neptune. At its present speed it would not reach Earth for several months. But if Burrow could not stop it, he had high confidence in the *Resolve*'s ability to destroy the mega-ship. The risks were acceptable to Barrett.

"Permission granted, Lieutenant Burrow," General Barrett decided. "But I'm sending reinforcements."

Burrow knew the general meant that he was sending Burrow's teammates from Bug Team Alpha. They were an elite special ops force within the Colonial Armed Forces. They answered only to General Barrett and the president of the Earth Colonial Coalition. Not only were the soldiers of Bug Team Alpha trained for unique and unusual missions, their bodies were specially designed for it. Each member had a different insect's DNA grafted onto his or her human DNA. This gave each of them superpowered buglike appearances and abilities.

"Thank you, sir," Burrow replied. "We'll get the job done, sir."

CHAPTER 2

As soon as General Barrett closed out the communications with Burrow and Addo, he pulled up the records for Bug Team Alpha. From a roster of nine members, the general selected five who would join Lt Burrow on the revised mission.

— — — — — — — — —

Commander Ariel "Dragonfly" Carter. Dragonfly wing DNA graft. High-velocity flight.

— — — — — — — — —

Lt Sancho "Locust" Castillo. Wing and back carapace DNA graft. Heavy-duty flight and strength.

— — — — — — — — —

Lt Irene "Impact" Mallory. Beetle exoskeleton DNA graft. High-impact tolerance and strength.

— — — — — — — — —

Lt Akiko "Radar" Murasaki. Cranial antennae DNA graft. Vibration detection.

Lt Madhuri "Scorpion" Singh. Scorpion spike DNA graft. Scorpion venom modified to knock out enemy, not poison.

When General Barrett finalized his choices, he sent out an Action Alert to the team's personal wrist computers. Bug Team Alpha was mobilized.

Twenty Earth Standard minutes later, Commander Ariel "Dragonfly" Carter and her team were geared up. They assembled in the space dock of Space Station Prime. The station was not only the headquarters for General Barrett and the Colonial Armed Forces. It was also the home base of Bug Team Alpha. Response time was immediate.

"The mission specs are pretty clear. We find a way into the mega-ship and stop it from hitting Earth," Dragonfly said as Bug Team Alpha boarded the *Arion*.

The *Arion* was a Zip Ship, a small but extremely fast spacecraft. Travel time to the *Resolve* through hyperspace would be under thirty minutes.

"So, we have to save Earth again. No pressure," Lt Madhuri "Scorpion" Singh joked.

"No problem," Lt Irene "Impact" Mallory assured her teammate. "We've got this."

Lt Akiko "Radar" Murasaki studied images of the mega-ship on her wrist computer. She whistled. "Burrow sure dug up a whopper," she added.

"No surprise there. That big bug is always getting into trouble," Lt Sancho "Locust" Castillo agreed.

Commander Dragonfly took the pilot's seat. As she fired up the ship's engines, the rest of the team stowed away their packs. Inside were the team's custom-fitted space suits they'd need for the mission. Standard suits and equipment could not be used. There was nothing standard about Bug Team Alpha.

"We have clearance from Dock Control," Dragonfly announced. "Launching in ten … nine … eight…"

A few seconds later the Zip Ship shot away from Space Station Prime. The members of Bug Team Alpha sped towards the edge of the solar system.

✳ ✳ ✳

Twenty-six minutes after departure, the *Arion* dropped out of hyperspace near the coordinates of the *Resolve*. The Bug Team members crowded into the cockpit to get their first look at the mega-ship.

"It's as big as a moon!" Radar said in awe.

"The technology it took to construct that thing must be amazing," Locust added. "Maybe we'll be able to salvage some of it."

"We need to get inside and put on the brakes first," Dragonfly reminded them. "Otherwise the *Resolve* is going to blast it into space dust."

The Bug Team wasted no time picking up Burrow from the *Resolve*. Even though the asteroid ship would not reach Earth for months, Bug Team Alpha had its own mission timetable. Their speciality was to get in, get the job done and get out. Then it was on to the next op.

Once they had the full team, Commander Dragonfly landed the *Arion* onto the copper-coloured hull of the mega-ship. The team helped one another put on their customized space suits. Dragonfly and Locust needed suits that had room for their wings. Impact's extra-large body and bug exoskeleton required an extra-large suit. Burrow climbed into his experimental armour.

Soon everyone was sealed up. They clipped blasters to their suits and strapped on combat belts. The belts held extra power packs and other gear. Each team member gave a thumbs-up. Bug Team Alpha was ready.

Dragonfly released the air from the ship. Then she opened the *Arion*'s hatch to the sunless vacuum of space.

"Helmet lights on," the commander ordered as they stepped out onto the mega-ship's hull.

Burrow pointed. "The nearest hatch is just over there," he said.

"Lead the way," Dragonfly instructed.

The team walked carefully over the metal. If any of them took a step that was too strong in the weak gravity, they risked pushing themselves off the surface. The two strongest teammates, Impact and Burrow, looked like they were tiptoeing on eggshells.

When the team reached the hatch, Dragonfly bent down to examine it. There was a pair of small touch pads on one side. One pad glowed with a dull purple light.

"The tech guys think it's a simple on and off switch," Burrow explained.

"There's only one way to find out," Dragonfly stated. She pressed the glowing purple pad.

Air gushed out as the hatch door dropped a few centimetres. Then the door slid sideways and out of sight. It revealed an opening.

The Bug Team directed their helmet lights down into the darkness. "It looks like an air lock chamber," Locust observed.

"Agreed. Let's go," Dragonfly said.

The commander stepped out over the opening. She did not fall. Instead, the light gravity slowly pulled her down into the air lock below. The team followed her.

When they had reached the bottom, their helmet lights revealed a small chamber. Two more touch pads were on the wall. One of them glowed a faint pink.

"Hmmm. Purple for 'open' and pink for 'close'?" Dragonfly wondered aloud. She pressed the pink touch pad. The hatch above their heads closed. "So far, so good."

Then suddenly the whole chamber moved out from under their feet.

CHAPTER 3

Bug Team Alpha floated in midair for a moment in the light gravity. Then the ceiling of the chamber came down to meet them. The whole chamber was moving downward. The soldiers were pressed flat against the closed hatch.

The chamber continued to go down, taking the Bug Team with it. "I guess this air lock is also a type of lift," Locust said.

The Bug Team felt the pull of an increasing gravity field as they went deeper into the ship. But they did not drop down to the floor. Instead, they stayed where they were. The chamber's ceiling had become the floor.

"Are we … upside down?" Impact asked.

"No, we're right side up. Down just became up," Burrow answered. He got to his feet and stood on the hatch. The rest of the team climbed to their feet too.

"Ugh… My stomach doesn't agree with you," Radar moaned.

"Just keep looking at your feet," Dragonfly said. "You'll adjust."

Radar kept her eyes down and concentrated on the readouts on her wrist computer. "Commander, suit sensors show the air lock is filling with an atmosphere," she reported. "It's Earth-compatible."

The air lock lift came to a stop. On the wall, a previously unseen hatch opened automatically.

Dragonfly unclipped her blaster. The rest of the team did the same. They braced for whatever lay beyond the door. Bug Team Alpha stepped out of the chamber.

"Whoa," Scorpion said.

"I've never seen anything like this," Impact added.

The team was in what looked like a warehouse district. Large, square buildings surrounded them on all sides. That seemed normal enough. But above their heads was something incredible.

Where they expected to see a ceiling, they saw the opposite side of the spherical mega-ship curving far overhead. Buildings hung down from the inside surface of the sphere like stalactites in a cave.

"The ship is *hollow*," Commander Dragonfly noted with surprise.

"And the inside is completely lined with structures. This is a very unusual ship," Locust said.

Floating in the "sky" in the centre of the sphere was a gigantic copper-coloured cube. A ring of bright globes surrounded the cube, lighting up the ship's interior. Closer to the ground were rows of smaller glowing orbs. They stretched out like streetlights down a road.

"We're inside some form of Dyson sphere – an inverted world," the commander said. "That lift didn't just serve as an air lock. It reoriented us from a surface that curves outwards to one that curves inwards."

"So it's just like Burrow said. Up became down," Impact said. "Thank goodness for artificial gravity."

Dragonfly tapped the comm button on her suit. "Commander Dragonfly to Captain Addo. We've successfully entered the mega-ship," she transmitted. She got static for a reply.

"The *Resolve*'s sensors couldn't get through the hull. I guess our comm signals can't either," Burrow said.

Dragonfly closed the channel. "OK, we're comm silent. Let's get out of these suits," she ordered.

The space suits weren't necessary inside the mega-ship. The air was breathable. Plus, the heavy gear got in the way of Bug Team Alpha's special abilities. As they removed the suits, the team buckled their blasters and combat belts to their mission armour.

Radar removed her helmet and flexed her antennae. "I'm not getting any vibes," she said as she scanned the area for sound and movement.

"Be on alert," the commander ordered. "Just because there aren't signs of life, doesn't mean there isn't any. Impact and Scorpion, scout left of the air lock. Burrow and Radar, scout right. Locust and I will fly aerial recon."

"Yes, ma'am!" the team responded in a unified voice.

Burrow, Radar, Impact and Scorpion shouldered their weapons. They split into two teams and headed out. Dragonfly launched up into the air. Locust quickly followed behind her.

The duo flew up about twenty metres. A sea of rooftops stretched out below them. The structures were laid out in a grid pattern and separated by roads and streets. All of them were empty.

"There's no traffic. No people that I can see," Locust told the commander.

"Maybe Burrow was right. This ship might be an abandoned relic," Dragonfly replied.

The commander and Locust flew higher for a wider view. The industrial section was extremely large, but there were structures beyond the warehouses. Dragonfly spotted buildings that looked like houses. They saw patches of green parkland. A flock of birds flew nearby.

"There are some living things, at least. I guess the ship isn't totally dead," Locust observed.

Something else caught Dragonfly's eye. "What's that?" she asked, pointing along the curve of the sphere.

Locust looked in the direction she was pointing. A massive structure rose hundreds of metres above the interior surface of the sphere. It looked like an enormous pile of black cubes.

"I don't know, but it's big," Locust replied.

Dragonfly tapped her wrist computer. She brought up the surface terrain map the *Resolve* had created. "It's at the same coordinates as the mountains," she said. "The mountains that are actually engine exhaust ports."

"Then those cubes must be the engine assembly!" Locust realized.

"There would probably be a control station in an engine assembly," Dragonfly noted. "We could use it to put on the brakes."

Then she looked up at the giant, copper-coloured cube floating in the centre of the sphere. "But I'd guess the ship's main controls are in there."

"That would make sense. Central cube. Central control," Locust agreed.

"The cube is closer than the assembly, so we'll check it out first," Dragonfly decided. "It must be at least twenty kilometres away, though. How fast can you fly?"

Locust revved his wings. They made a low hum.

Dragonfly grinned. "Nice to know you'll be able to keep up with me," she said.

Before they started, the commander contacted the rest of her team on the comm. "Commander Dragonfly to Bug Team. Locust and I are going to investigate the central cube. Report your status."

The reply was a confusion of shouts and blaster fire.

"The team is under attack!" Dragonfly exclaimed.

"From who?" Locust asked. "I thought this was an abandoned ship."

"Maybe not," Dragonfly replied grimly.

Commander Dragonfly and Lt Locust buzzed back towards the surface at full speed. They could hear the sharp sounds of blaster fire. Bright energy flares flashed in the distance.

Dragonfly checked the scouting teams' location signals on her wrist computer. "They're being engaged in two locations," she said. "Locust, provide backup for Impact and Scorpion. I'll help Burrow and Radar. Break!"

The two airborne soldiers peeled off from each other and dived towards their friends. Dragonfly could see that Burrow and Radar were caught in the open streets. There was no cover except for the warehouses, and those were all sealed. The two teammates ran in evasive zigzags. They turned back now and then to fire at the enemy.

Dragonfly squeezed her blaster trigger and provided a round of covering fire. That was when she saw what was attacking her team.

In the other location, Locust made the same realization. "Robots!" he exclaimed over the comm.

Each scouting team was being pursued by large, copper-coloured robots. They stomped after the Bug Team

members on thick mechanical legs. Powerful bursts of energy shot out from their blaster arms.

One of the three robots attacking Radar and Burrow suddenly stopped. Its small round head swivelled towards the sky. It tracked Dragonfly as she zoomed overhead. The robot began firing.

"They're probably automatic security drones," Dragonfly said, smoothly dodging the blasts. "We must have triggered them when we opened the air lock."

"All I know is that our blasters have no effect on them," Burrow told Dragonfly over the comm. "And it looks like they're made from the same alloy as the ship's hull. Which means…"

"Which means the hull might be resistant to the *Resolve*'s weapons too," Dragonfly finished. "This ship might be tougher to destroy than we thought."

The commander fired her blaster at the robots as she swooped down again and again. Despite the combined firepower of Dragonfly, Burrow and Radar, the robots shrugged off the assault.

"This is useless," Radar growled. "We can't stop them!"

CHAPTER 4

Impact, Scorpion and Locust battled two other robots with as little success as Dragonfly, Burrow and Radar. Their blaster shots bounced off the robots' metal bodies.

This began to annoy Impact. "I've had it with these clanking drones!" she shouted suddenly. She ran straight at the robots like a charging bull.

"Impact! What are you –" Scorpion started to say, then stopped. "Oh." She watched as Impact barrelled into the security drones like a bowling ball through a line of pins.

The robots toppled over. Before the machines could get up, Impact took a small grenade from her combat belt. She slapped it onto the chest of one of the robots. As the lieutenant ran away, she mouthed a countdown.

"Zero," she finished. The grenade – and the robot – exploded in a bright flash.

Impact casually walked over to the second robot. It was disabled from the nearby explosion, but not deactivated. Impact made sure that it was.

Locust landed next to the busted robots. "That was either really brave or really stupid," he said.

"I'd call it effective," Impact replied.

"At least now we know how to stop these things," Scorpion said as she joined them.

"The commander will want to know about this. Locust to Dragonfly," Locust reported over the comm. "Impact took out one of the robots with a grenade. A point-blank blast will destroy them."

"Good work!" Commander Dragonfly replied. "We're taking action now."

A moment later the three teammates heard a loud *boom*. The sound of blaster fire stopped instantly.

"I guess they got 'em," Impact said.

Dragonfly's voice came over the comm. "Locust, Scorpion, Impact, meet at my location," she ordered. "I need to brief you all on what Locust and I discovered on aerial recon."

"Yes, ma'am," they replied.

Locust brought up the commander's location on his wrist computer. The three started towards the rest of Bug Team Alpha.

Impact, Locust and Scorpion walked through the empty streets of the warehouse district. Nothing broke the silence around them. It was almost too quiet. The doors to every building they passed were shut and sealed. There were no vehicles parked on the streets. No random bits of rubbish. No skittering of vermin.

"This place is too clean," Scorpion whispered to the others. "I don't like it."

"Maybe the robots weren't security drones. Maybe they were vacuum cleaners," Impact joked. "They just thought we were a mess to clean up."

"Well, we sure made a mess out of those robots," Locust replied.

The trio turned a corner. Their comrades were standing at the end of the street. The remains of three robots littered the floor nearby.

Impact walked up and kicked one of the destroyed machines. "Vacuum cleaner," she muttered.

"OK, team. Listen up," Commander Dragonfly began. "The main bridge is probably located in that giant cube in the sky. I was going to investigate, but the robot attack has changed things. Locust and I can't leave the rest of you on the ground. You were attacked once. It could happen again."

"We can handle any drones," Impact argued.

"Maybe, but we spotted the ship's engine assembly. It's logical that a control room is located there, and it's easier to reach than the cube. Best tactic is to attack the easiest target," Dragonfly said. "The good news is we should be able to use the control room to stop the ship. The bad news is it's about forty kilometres away."

"That's a hike," Radar noted.

"That's why we're going to search for vehicles first. There's got to be something in one of the warehouses," Dragonfly said. She turned and shot the mechanical lock off the large warehouse doors behind her. "We'll start the search with this building right here. Burrow, Impact, crack the door."

The two muscular teammates had no trouble pulling the huge pair of doors aside. Bug Team Alpha faced the dark opening with blasters raised and ready.

Radar scanned the black interior with her antennae. "No movement," she reported.

The Bug Team stepped through the doors. The light from outside reached only a few metres inside. That was enough for Commander Dragonfly to locate a touch pad that turned on the warehouse lights.

The lights revealed a warehouse filled to its roof with huge metal crates. Each one was three metres tall and about the size of a small spacecraft. Alien writing was stamped uniformly on the sides.

"Open one up," the commander ordered. "Let's see what's inside."

Impact climbed on top of a container. She easily hauled off the heavy lid. "More boxes," she said.

Dragonfly buzzed up and landed beside Impact. She opened one of the boxes that was tightly packed in the crate. Inside were packages made from a lightweight material she could not identify. It wasn't cardboard. It wasn't metal. However, it was easy to open.

She examined the contents. "It looks like an MRE – Meal, Ready-to-Eat," Dragonfly said. "It's food."

"Lots and lots of it," Scorpion said, gazing at the hundreds of crates inside the warehouse.

"But who is it all for? Isn't the ship abandoned?" Impact asked.

"I guess the food was abandoned too," Dragonfly said. "Let's just hope they left behind a couple of lorries that we can use."

The team explored more warehouses. Some stored vast amounts of food. Others stored huge tanks of water. Dragonfly estimated there were enough supplies to sustain a large population for hundreds of years. And yet they saw no sign that people still lived on the ship.

"This is kind of spooky – all this stuff and nobody around to use it," Locust said as the team searched through yet another building. "It's like a ghost town."

Bug Team Alpha's search took them from the warehouse district into a manufacturing area. The team began exploring a foundry. Half-constructed robots hung from overhead conveyor lines. Giant vats for smelting and processing metal were stopped along their tracks. Large channels in the floor connected a series of deep pit moulds used to shape the robots' metallic bodies. The factory was as quiet as a graveyard.

And then they heard a scream.

CHAPTER 5

Bug Team Alpha reacted to the sound of the scream as if it had been a blaster shot.

Commander Dragonfly launched into the air for recon. Locust buzzed beside her.

The rest of the team fell into a wedge formation with blasters drawn. They followed their aerial leaders further into the factory.

"I'm getting vibes!" Radar cautioned over the comm. "Movement, thirty metres ahead."

The Bug Team members on the ground moved quietly and with extreme caution. Dragonfly and Locust flew as silently as they could through the hanging conveyor cables and vats.

Commander Dragonfly was preparing for another wave of defence drones. Her hand reached towards the grenades on her combat belt.

"I'm going to have visual in three … two… What?" Dragonfly gasped. "Stand down! Stand down! Bug Team Alpha, do not fire!"

The team members immediately lifted their blasters away from their shoulders. What they had in their sights were not hostile drones.

"*Kids?*" Burrow exclaimed.

A group of humanoid children dressed in tan jumpsuits whirled around. They were standing next to the edge of a pit in the factory floor. As soon as they saw the Bug Team, they shrieked and ran. A desperate cry came up from the pit.

"Locust, follow them. But don't engage," Dragonfly ordered. "Obviously this ship is not as abandoned as we thought."

As Locust flew after the kids, Dragonfly hovered over the pit. She saw a child standing at the bottom. He was trying to climb up the smooth sides of the hole, without success. He let out an angry yell. Then he saw Commander Dragonfly.

"Yaaaa!" the child shrieked. He cowered on the floor of the pit.

The rest of the Bug Team peered over the edge.

"Hmph. The kids were probably playing where they didn't belong. Then this one got into trouble," Impact said.

"Ha! Don't tell me you never did the same thing when you were little," Burrow joked. He nudged his teammate with a spiked elbow.

Impact snorted. "I was an angel until I joined Bug Team Alpha," she replied.

"That's enough chatter. The kid is scared," Dragonfly ordered. She descended slowly into the pit and spoke in a calm voice to the child. "It's OK. I'm here to help."

Dragonfly landed next to him. She saw the child was humanoid with smooth, tan skin. Two small horns extended out from his forehead. Dragonfly reached out a hand.

"I can get you out of here," the commander said. She fluttered her wings gently.

The kid pressed himself against the wall and wrapped his arms around his head.

Dragonfly sighed. It was obvious the child was too afraid to cooperate. "All right, I won't force you to be rescued," she said.

The commander flew out of the pit and rejoined the others. "All right, Bug Team. Let's move out," Dragonfly ordered.

"We're not going to just abandon the kid, are we?" Radar protested.

The commander gave Radar a steely look. "Are you questioning my order, Lieutenant?" she said sharply.

"No, ma'am!" Radar responded.

"Then move out," Dragonfly repeated.

Radar glanced back at the pit, but she followed the order. Bug Team Alpha left the building.

As they did, Dragonfly buzzed up to one of the conveyor cables. She cut off a section with her combat knife. Then she tied one end around some nearby railings and dropped the other end into the pit.

Bug Team Alpha needed to continue with its mission. But the cable would give the child a way to climb out and rescue himself.

"You can do it, kid," Dragonfly whispered.

As Commander Dragonfly buzzed out of the foundry building to rejoin her team, a sudden realization hit her. There were *people* on this ship – a ship that was on a collision course with Earth. If the Bug Team couldn't find a way to stop it, the ship was going to be destroyed. And all the people along with it. She had to find a way to warn the inhabitants about the danger they were in.

A voice over the comm interrupted Dragonfly's thoughts. "Commander, I followed the kids. They went home," Locust reported. "Remember the structures we saw earlier, the ones that looked like houses? Turns out it was a village."

"So there *is* a surviving community on this ship," Dragonfly said. The mission was definitely getting complicated.

"The kids must have raised an alarm," Locust added. "I count fourteen security robots heading in your direction."

"Destroying their security force is not the way I want to have our first meeting with these people," the commander said. She shook her head. "But sometimes I just don't get what I want."

Commander Dragonfly recalled Lt Locust and ordered her team to prepare for another drone attack. There was no way to avoid contact. There was only one road between the industrial and residential districts. An open park separated the two areas like a grassy neutral zone. It was about to become a battlefield.

The ground members of the Bug Team marched down the road in a wedge formation. Dragonfly and Locust flew ahead of their other teammates. Everyone held blasters at the ready. In the distance, Commander Dragonfly could see the approaching robots.

Suddenly Radar's antennae twitched. "Movement on the right!" she warned.

Bug Team Alpha prepared for an ambush. But it wasn't an enemy force. It was the kid from the pit. He ran across the field towards the robots.

"I knew he could do it," Dragonfly said quietly. Then she saw the new danger he was in. "Oh no. Get out of the line of fire, kid!"

The robots had raised their blaster arms. They were taking aim at the boy.

"No!" Dragonfly shouted. She shot at the line of security drones. "Bug Team Alpha, engage! Draw fire away from the kid!"

The team opened fire and broke into a sprint towards the drones. The robots fired back at the Bug Team. Their attention was no longer on the child.

"Locust! Strafing run!" Dragonfly ordered.

The two aerial members of Bug Team Alpha swooped down in unison. The commander knew their weapons would not damage the enemy. Instead, she and Locust blasted the road in front of the robots. It created a cloud of dust and debris.

The rest of Bug Team Alpha used it as cover to engage their opponents. They surged forward.

"Pick a target and deploy grenades," Commander Dragonfly instructed.

The half-human, half-bug soldiers were fast on their feet – much faster than the robots, with their heavy mechanical legs. Impact and Burrow each barrelled into a pair of drones. The robots tumbled over. The two teammates slapped grenades onto the drones' metal torsos and kept on running.

Scorpion and Radar slid between another pair of robots and planted their charges from below. Locust slammed his heels into two more machines. They fell with a thud. Locust landed on their chest plates long enough to attach grenades.

While her team engaged the drones, Dragonfly buzzed at top speed towards the boy. He stood frozen with fear, right in the middle of the danger zone.

CHAPTER 6

Blaster fire followed Commander Dragonfly as she flew towards the terrified child. She rolled and zigzagged away from the shots. This time the commander ignored the child's fear of her. She scooped him into her arms. Together, they sped upwards into the artificial sky, away from the battle.

BOOOOM! BOOOOM! BOOOOM!

Dragonfly heard the explosions as the grenades detonated. Blaster fire continued for a short while as the remaining robots fought the Bug Team.

BOOM! BOOOOM!

Silence.

"The enemy is neutralized," Locust reported over the comm.

"Good work, team," Dragonfly replied. "I'm taking the kid into the village. Meet me there."

The commander glided towards the residential area. The child relaxed in her arms. She thought he might have fainted. But as soon as she landed, the kid ran off.

Dragonfly sighed and looked around. She had touched down in a park-like section of the residential district. Large, tree-like plants and small shrubs dotted the grassy field. She heard the song of birds. Dragonfly wondered if they were the ones that she and Locust had seen earlier.

Then the commander saw a vehicle. It was parked at the edge of the grass.

"Finally!" Dragonfly exclaimed. She buzzed over to the sturdy little service lorry. It had an open cargo platform in the back and a tiny driver's cabin. The commander doubted that anyone larger than Radar would be able to fit into the cab. But it would do.

"Commander!"

Dragonfly turned at the sound of Impact's voice. Bug Team Alpha was walking over. But they weren't alone.

"Commander, the townspeople have come out to say hello," Impact said sarcastically.

The Bug Team members had their hands in the air. Behind them was a crowd of humanoids all dressed in tan jumpsuits. Horns curved out from their tan foreheads. The commander realized they were the adult version of the kid she had saved. They all held weapons.

Dragonfly put up her hands. "Not the sort of first meeting I wanted at all…"

As the townspeople herded the Bug Team towards Commander Dragonfly, she noticed no one had taken the soldiers' blasters or combat belts. And the citizens weren't actually pointing their weapons at the team.

Dragonfly hoped these were signs that the people were peaceful. Then she noticed something else as the townspeople silently surrounded them.

"These people all look the same. Exactly the same. Identical," Dragonfly whispered.

Impact studied the features of their captors. "What, like twins?" she asked quietly.

"More like triplets, or even septuplets," Scorpion said.

"More like clones," Dragonfly concluded.

"They could be androids," Locust suggested. "They could be mechanical, like the robots. Only with better tech, and better looking."

"But what about the kid I saved? Why make android children?" Dragonfly argued. "Anyway, it doesn't matter if they're clones or androids or anything in between. They're in danger."

The commander stepped forward. "People!" she said to the crowd. "This ship is on a collision course with a planet called Earth. Everyone on board is in danger!"

Dragonfly's dramatic statement did not get the shocked reaction she was expecting. No one reacted at all. No one spoke. They all stared at the Bug Team with blank eyes.

"See? Androids," Locust whispered.

"This ship is heading straight towards an inhabited planet – our home," Dragonfly explained to the crowd. "We've been sent here to stop the ship. Help us. Help yourselves."

"We will not collide –" one person began.

"– with the planet Earth," another finished.

"It is our –"

"– destination."

The clones spoke individually. But they spoke with one thought, one message.

"They're not just clones," Commander Dragonfly realized. "They must have a hive mind. They're all connected."

Burrow eyed the clones suspiciously. "What, like one giant brain in a whole bunch of bodies?" he asked.

Scorpion shook her head. "Think of it as a bee hive. All the bees are mentally connected and act as a single unit," she explained.

Dragonfly turned her attention back towards their captors. "You said Earth is your destination. Do you mean that this ship is heading there on purpose?" she asked.

"The planet has been selected –"

"– for harvest."

"That doesn't sound good," Burrow muttered.

"Tell me about this 'harvest,'" Dragonfly said to the clones.

"We cannot respond in that area," the clones replied as a unit.

The commander sighed. "All right. What is your function on this ship?"

"We sort and store."

"The warehouse district was full of food and supplies," Radar whispered. "They must be the workers."

"But if they only sort and store, who does the harvesting?" Dragonfly wondered.

The clones heard the commander's question. "We cannot respond in that area," they said.

"Well, who *can* respond?" Scorpion asked.

All the clones looked up to the giant metal cube in the sky.

"It's just as you thought, Commander. Central cube. Central control," Locust said.

"Is the ship's bridge in that cube?" Dragonfly asked.

"We cannot respond in –"

Suddenly the clones stopped in mid-reply. Their expressions changed. They looked as if their previous thought had been interrupted. Now they were listening to a new one. All at once, each clone lifted his or her weapon. They pointed them at the Bug Team.

"Uh-oh," Radar said. She and the rest of the team raised their blasters in response.

Commander Dragonfly held up a hand. "Hold your fire," she ordered.

The two groups stared at each other. Neither made a move.

"Now what?" Locust whispered.

The lieutenant's question was answered by the sound of blaring alarms. In the artificial sky, the rows of light orbs started to shift. They rearranged into grids, creating giant monitors.

The clones turned their gaze upwards. Alien writing scrolled across the newly formed screens. A navigational space map of a sun with the orbits of eight planetary bodies appeared. A copper-coloured dot crossed the outermost orbit.

Dragonfly's eyes grew wide. "That's our solar system," she realized.

"Target planet detected. Engines engaged. Prepare for acceleration," a voice announced.

Bug Team Alpha felt the ground vibrate. A distant roar echoed throughout the ship.

Radar's antennae twitched. "The vibes are coming from the engine assembly. It's activating!" she exclaimed.

Moments later the mega-ship's engines came to life. The floor lurched under their feet. Despite the warning, the clones stumbled. Bug Team Alpha used the distraction to escape.

"Head for that lorry!" Commander Dragonfly yelled, flying towards the little vehicle she had spotted earlier. "We have to get to the engine assembly. We have to shut it down before this ship gets to Earth!"

Bug Team Alpha's timetable had suddenly accelerated, just like the mega-ship.

CHAPTER 7

Aboard the destroyer-class spacecraft *Resolve*, alarms sounded the call to battle stations. The giant asteroid ship had suddenly started to accelerate. It was heading straight for the destroyer. The *Resolve*'s pilot scrambled to move the ship out of the way.

"Is Bug Team Alpha doing this?" Captain Addo asked angrily. "There's been nothing but comm silence for the past three hours. And now this. They were supposed to stop the mega-ship, not speed it up!"

"At least now we know what the ship uses for propulsion," Lt Dianna Dennis announced. She stood at the main sensor station on the bridge. Her biomechanical hands tapped the station's touchscreen. "It's a magnetic soliton pulse."

Addo frowned. "A what?"

"A soliton is a type of wave that holds its shape over long distances. This one is made of magnetic energy," Lt Dennis explained. "That's why we couldn't find any energy residue. It's a very clean form of propulsion."

"A wave, huh? Do you mean that the mega-ship is using it to surf?" the captain asked.

"Sort of. The ship is being pushed by the wave," Lt Dennis replied. "It's moving at incredible speed."

Addo frowned. "Is it still on course for Earth?"

"Yes, sir. Arrival is now calculated to be in fifty-seven Earth Standard hours," Lt Dennis said.

"I have to report this to General Barrett," the captain said. He opened up a communications channel. "The mission parameters have just turned critical."

✳   ✳   ✳

General Barrett paced back and forth in his office aboard Space Station Prime. He had just received Captain Addo's report.

"So, our countdown went from months to hours," the general growled. "Target the engine exhaust ports.

Knocking them out may stop the mega-ship. I don't want to lose Bug Team Alpha if it can be helped. If that has no effect, you have orders to destroy the ship. Even if the Bug Team is still on board."

"Understood, sir," Addo said. "And if that proves unsuccessful…?"

The captain let the statement hang.

"I want another report in thirty Earth Standard minutes," Barrett ordered.

After the captain of the *Resolve* signed off, the general began his own preparations. He was assembling an armada of destroyers and battleships. He needed to be ready with reinforcements – just in case the *Resolve* failed to stop the juggernaut headed towards Earth.

Inside the mega-ship, Bug Team Alpha sped down a wide road in the little service lorry. Burrow, Impact and Scorpion rode on the cargo platform. Radar was driving. She was the only one small enough to fit in the tiny cab. Dragonfly and Locust flew overhead.

No one had come after them. No one paid any attention to the strange sight of the superpowered soldiers as they drove towards the assembly. The clones all seemed focused on other tasks now.

"More vehicles are coming onto the road up ahead. Traffic is increasing," the commander told the team over the comm. "This ship is waking up."

"But why now?" Locust asked. "It was so inactive before that we thought it was an abandoned relic."

"That announcement said the target planet had been detected. Maybe that started things moving," Radar suggested.

"That target planet is Earth, right?" Scorpion asked. "And the clones said something about a harvest…"

"What are you getting at, Lieutenant?" Dragonfly prompted.

"What if Earth is going to be harvested?" Scorpion concluded. "How do you even harvest a planet? It can't be a good thing."

"That's what I said," Burrow muttered.

Dragonfly cut in. "All the more reason to get to the engine assembly and stop this ship."

Radar pushed the vehicle to its top speed. The black bulk of the engine assembly loomed closer and closer.

"I can feel the vibes of the assembly," Radar reported. "I can't tell what kind of energy it's generating. But it's low frequency and very powerful."

Dragonfly and Locust watched from the air as more traffic streamed towards the enormous structure. Every vehicle contained clones. But these clones were different. They all had red skin and horns curved like ram horns.

"Looks like we've got another type of clone heading for the assembly," Dragonfly said.

"A different clone type for a different function?" Locust guessed.

"It would seem that way," Dragonfly agreed.

The Bug Team's little vehicle blended into the masses as it entered the district.

"The external engine assembly has been targeted, sir. Torpedoes locked," the weapons officer aboard the *Resolve* informed Captain Addo.

"You may fire when ready," Addo ordered.

"Firing now, sir," the officer announced.

Six energy torpedoes launched from the *Resolve*. They sailed towards the "mountains" on the asteroid mega-ship. On the bridge, Captain Addo watched their course on the tactical monitors.

The weapons officer counted down. "Impact in eight … six … two… Impact!"

"Magnify image on tac-four," Addo ordered. He wanted to have a real-eye visual of the destruction, not a chart.

The tac-four monitor zoomed in. The display filled with massive clouds of dust. The mountains were invisible in the swirling debris.

"Come on, come on," the captain muttered. He was impatient for the clouds to clear and reveal success.

The weak gravity could not hold onto the dust any longer. The bits of rock and rubble were left behind as the mega-ship continued to move through space. Gradually, the results of the *Resolve*'s torpedoes were unveiled.

Inside the giant engine assembly structure, Bug Team Alpha felt the impact of the torpedoes hitting the mega-ship's exterior. The floor under their feet shook like small earthquakes. Six times.

"I recognize those vibes! They're from Coalition torpedoes," Radar declared. "The *Resolve* is firing on us!"

Commander Dragonfly frowned. Her team was running out of time. "They have to. This ship accelerated, and we haven't done anything to stop it."

Bug Team Alpha had left the lorry. They were now inside the assembly and moving on foot through the tight corridors. The commander led the search for the engine control room. Once they found it, they should be able to power down the ship.

The red-skinned clone workers did not seem to notice the Bug Team running among them. They barely reacted to the torpedo impacts. They carried out their assigned tasks, even as the floors and walls trembled.

Impact sidestepped a clone who was about to walk straight into her. She shook her head. "The hive mind makes them act just like the robot drones."

The team continued to race through the maze of corridors. It started to feel like they were going in circles.

"I'm picking up major vibes ahead," Radar suddenly announced. "They've got to be coming from the engine generator, and the engine control room should be near the generator. We're close."

"Lead the way," the commander instructed.

Radar stepped to the front. Using her antennae, she followed the increasing vibrations. Soon, she guided the team to a huge open chamber.

Dragonfly quickly scanned the room. There weren't any clone workers. There was only one enormous, yet simple, device.

In the centre of the round chamber stood a structure that looked like three tall, thick mushrooms. Ribbons of lightning stabbed out from the tops and arced across the curved ceiling. The bolts of raw energy roared like never-ending thunder. This was the machine that powered the mega-ship.

"OK, team," Commander Dragonfly said. "Time to find the off switch."

CHAPTER 8

Aboard the *Resolve*, Captain Addo watched the dust disappear from the surface of the asteroid ship. He did not like what he saw. The rock was blasted away, but the coppery metal of the exhaust ports was still intact.

"Not a scratch! What's that ship made of?" the captain growled.

"I still can't identify the alloy, sir," Lt Dennis reported from her sensor station.

"Prepare to fire again. Increase to twelve torpedoes. Follow up with plasma cannons," Addo ordered.

The *Resolve* hurled a second wave of firepower at the mega-ship. The explosions looked like a small sun. But when the blaze faded, the engine exhaust ports were still undamaged. The ship continued to hurtle towards Earth.

"Open a comm channel to General Barrett," the captain instructed grimly.

Inside the mega-ship, the members of Bug Team Alpha was nearly knocked off their feet by the barrage unleashed by the *Resolve*. Streams of energy continued to arc from the generator. The *Resolve*'s attack had no effect.

"That was right on top of us," Radar said as she uncurled her antennae. The vibrations from the blast had been so strong they were painful.

"They're not getting through the hull," Burrow observed. "The hull's metal alloy must be resistant to the *Resolve*'s weapons. Just like how our blasters didn't harm the robots."

"The robots had a weak spot, though. The alloy can be damaged," Commander Dragonfly reminded them. "But there's no way to tell that to the *Resolve*. It's up to us to stop this ship from the inside."

"We could blow up the generator," Impact suggested.

Locust shook his head. "It wouldn't do much good. Destroying the generator would cut power to the engines.

But the ship's momentum would still carry it on its course towards Earth. We have to find the brakes."

"Commander, I think I see the control room!" Scorpion shouted over the crackling lightning. She pointed to a small room on the opposite side of the chamber. It was barely a slot in the wall. But it was lined with active monitors and blinking lights.

Bug Team Alpha ran under the umbrella of energy and crowded into the little room. Rows of touch pads lined the walls with alien writing next to each.

"One of these controls has to stop the ship. All we have to do is find it," Dragonfly said. She started to press random touch pads.

"Or, we might accidentally hit the self-destruct button and blow up the ship," Impact mentioned.

"Well, then it's still mission accomplished," the commander replied.

The Bug Team followed Dragonfly's lead. They pushed every touch pad in reach. Out in the generator chamber, the twisting energy began to lessen. Soon, the roar had reduced to a murmur.

Scorpion stuck her head out of the control room to check the generator. "It's powering down!" she cheered.

Then she saw something else. "Uh-oh. Team, we've got incoming!"

A blur of security squads zoomed in on antigravity platforms. They were heading straight for the control room.

The Bug Team knew the danger of being caught in a small, confined space. "Spread out!" Commander Dragonfly ordered.

Bug Team Alpha surged out of the little room. But the moment they had the enemy in their blaster sights, they realized something. They were not facing ordinary robot drones.

"Cyborgs!" Locust exclaimed in surprise.

The security squads were made up of humanoids with cybernetic implants covering their bodies. Some had blasters for arms. Others had Taser claws instead of hands. None of them looked alike. None of them were clones. Each cyborg was a different alien species.

"Weapons on stun! These are living beings!" Dragonfly warned as the security squads opened fire.

"I don't recognize any of these species!" Radar yelled as she shot back. "Where are they from? How did they get on this ship?"

"Harvested!" Scorpion realized. "They must have been harvested from planets targeted by the mega-ship!"

Further speculation was not possible. The cyborgs surged forward. They wore armour made of the same coppery alloy as the robots and the ship's hull. It made no difference if the Bug Team's blasters were on max stun. Nothing could get through the alloy. And the team was not going to use grenades on living beings.

Commander Dragonfly could only see one option to disable the cyborgs without harming them permanently. "Locust, follow my lead!" she shouted. "Bug Team Alpha, cover me!"

Dragonfly spread her wings and buzzed towards one of the security squads. She dodged oncoming fire and slammed into a cyborg. Dragonfly grabbed it and twirled around like a tornado. Then she tossed the cyborg up into the weakening electric bolts coming from the generator.

ZAAAAP! The cyborg fell to the ground. The electricity had knocked the enemy unconscious, despite the alloy armour.

"I'm glad this time it's not the bugs getting zapped," Locust muttered to himself. He dove toward a cyborg and copied his commander's moves.

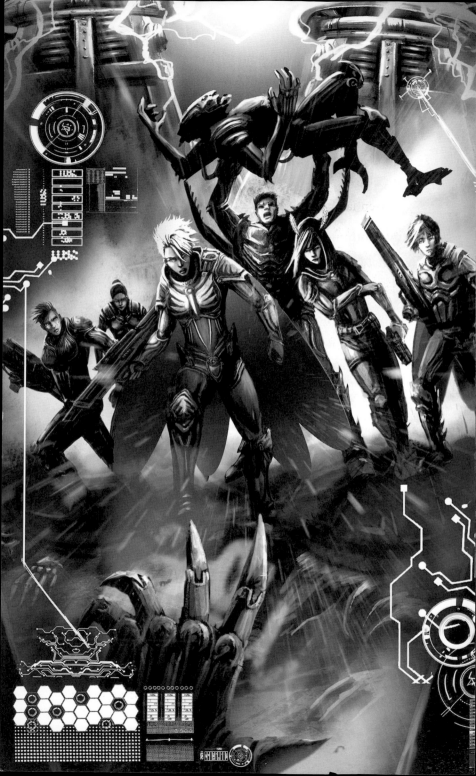

The rest of the team followed Dragonfly's lead. Radar used her vibration-sensitive antennae to anticipate the cyborgs' movements. She smoothly dodged their Taser claws. While Radar distracted the enemy, Impact and Burrow grabbed them from behind. Using their DNA-enhanced strength, they hurled the cyborgs up into the generator's energy field.

Amid the chaos, Scorpion targeted individual cyborgs. She ducked past her opponent's blaster fire. When she got close enough, she stabbed its skin with her thumb spikes. Soon she had taken down several cyborgs with her knockout venom.

In a matter of minutes, Burrow was throwing the last enemy into the energy field. The rest of the Bug Team carefully headed back to the control room. The floor was covered with knocked-out cyborgs. But just before one cyborg lost consciousness, it turned a mechanical eye on the soldiers. The lens zoomed in on Dragonfly.

"Identify yourself!" the cyborg ordered.

Dragonfly stood tall and proud. "I am Commander Dragonfly of Bug Team Alpha," she replied.

"You are Alpha?" a loud voice asked. The question came from the cyborgs, even though their bodies were unconscious. Someone else was speaking through the cyborgs' external comm system. Bug Team Alpha had faced many unusual foes, but this was a first.

"I thought these guys were cyborgs, not zombies," Burrow muttered.

"Yes. I am the leader of Bug Team Alpha," Dragonfly told the voice. "Your ship is heading directly for the planet Earth, our home. We've been sent to –"

The voice ignored her. "You are Alpha!" it declared. "The challenge has been accepted."

"Wait, what challenge? Who am I speaking to?" Dragonfly asked.

"I am the Alpha of the World Ship," the voice replied.

✳   ✳   ✳

General Barrett stood on the bridge of his flagship, the *Ares*, as it approached the asteroid ship. Following behind the *Ares* was an armada of four battleships, three destroyers and three fighter carriers. The general studied the mega-ship on a tactical monitor screen.

"So this is the nut that's been so hard to crack," Barrett said to himself.

"Captain Addo to General Barrett." The image of the *Resolve*'s captain appeared on a communications monitor screen. "The asteroid ship's engine has shut down. It's no longer accelerating."

"Then the armada's firepower was not needed after all. Good work, Captain," the general said.

Addo cleared his throat. "It wasn't anything the *Resolve* did, sir. The engine stopped by itself."

"Bug Team Alpha," Barrett concluded with a small smile of pride.

Addo didn't look so pleased. "Sir, the mega-ship's engine may have shut down, but the ship is still heading for Earth," he warned. "What are your orders?"

General Barrett trusted in the firepower of the armada to destroy the asteroid ship. But he also trusted in Bug Team Alpha.

Barrett opened a comm channel to the fleet. "All ships stand by," he instructed. He was willing to give his special ops team a little more time to complete their mission. But when that time was up, the Bug Team had to get off the mega-ship – or be destroyed along with it.

CHAPTER 9

Commander Dragonfly wasn't sure if the voice calling itself the Alpha of the World Ship was a person or a machine. It didn't matter to her at the moment. Bug Team Alpha had shut off the engines of the mega-ship, but it was still moving towards Earth.

"Search for navigation controls. We have to change this ship's course away from Earth," Dragonfly ordered.

The Bug Team went back to the control room. They had just begun trying the pads again when a squad of clones entered the room. These were not worker clones.

Bug Team Alpha faced a group of eight humanoid clones dressed in long robes. Four had dull blue skin and slim, twisted horns. The other four had mossy green skin and horns along their cheekbones. None were armed.

"Come. The Alpha Challenge awaits," the clones said.

"Where?" Dragonfly asked.

"Come. The Alpha Challenge awaits," the clones said again.

"They cannot respond in that area," Impact muttered sarcastically.

Commander Dragonfly allowed Bug Team Alpha to be guided out of the chamber. "I have no idea what this 'challenge' is, but I want to talk to whoever is in charge. They could stop this ship," Dragonfly told her soldiers. "And if that's the Alpha, then we go see the Alpha."

The Bug Team was taken to a sleek vehicle parked outside the engine assembly. Six of the clones got into the back of the vehicle with Bug Team Alpha. They did not try to take the teams' weapons. The other two clones climbed into the cockpit. A moment later the vehicle rose into the air.

The gigantic interior of the mega-ship curved all around them as they flew through the sky. Above their heads, the team spotted vast cities that looked as if they were hanging from the ceiling. To the left were the dense industrial districts. Small pockets of greenery and residential areas dotted the city landscape. Directly ahead of them loomed the floating copper-coloured cube. That was where they were headed.

The vehicle sped towards the cube. The surface looked smooth, with no obvious sign of an entrance. But a hatch opened just in time. Instead of crashing into the side of the cube, the vehicle flew into a tunnel.

They travelled through the dark tunnel for several more minutes. A light appeared ahead as the transport entered a large chamber. The vehicle touched down, and another group of clones crowded around it.

The vehicle's doors slid open automatically. Bug Team Alpha climbed out. The clones waiting for them stood in groups according to their skin colour and horn type. They all wore robes matching their skin colour – red, tan, blue and green.

The clones from the vehicle joined the others and surrounded the Bug Team. Then they started to march. The team had no choice but to move forward with the group. Up close, Dragonfly observed that the facial features of the red clones were different from the features of the green clones. It was as if they were copied from different sources.

"It looks like we have a variety of clone models here," the commander whispered to her team. "I guess there's genetic diversity after all. Or at least, there was at some point in the past."

The clones led Bug Team Alpha down a hall and into another chamber. This one was lavishly decorated. The floors were made from slabs of precious stones. Above, rare gems on the ceiling glittered like stars. Shelves and display cases covered the walls. Each was filled with artefacts from worlds unknown to the Bug Team. It was as if the chamber were a museum.

At the other end of the room stood another group of humanoids. There were twelve individuals, a male and a female of each colour: red, green, blue, tan, lavender and deep brown. None of them was dressed alike. Their clothing was very different from one another and from the robed clone escorts standing behind Bug Team Alpha.

"These must be the leaders. A male and female representative for each clone type," Scorpion said. "These people might even be the source of all the other clones."

Dragonfly barely nodded in response. Her attention wasn't on the court of clones. Her eyes went straight to the figure seated in the middle of them.

Sitting on what looked like a throne was a single male. He was tall and muscular, with black skin and four large, pointed horns. He was completely unique.

"The Alpha," Dragonfly whispered.

"What species are you?" the female with lavender skin and triple horns asked the Bug Team. She did not offer her own identity.

"We're humans from Earth," Dragonfly replied. "We've come to –"

"Humans are a very diverse species," interrupted the green-skinned male with curved horns.

"Too diverse," added the tan-skinned female.

"Their genetic lines are over-mixed," concluded one with blue skin and slim, twisting horns.

"I think we've just been insulted," Impact growled.

"Oh, we've been insulted," Burrow confirmed.

"Which of you is the Alpha?" asked the individual on the throne.

Dragonfly stepped forward. "I am," she declared. "And who are you?"

The black-skinned male abruptly stood up from the throne. He let out an angry roar.

"I think *he's* just been insulted," Impact said with a smile.

Burrow grinned. "Oh, he has definitely been insulted."

"I am Malrex, Alpha of the World Ship and Ancestor of the Ebon Genetic Line," the male announced. He stepped down from his throne. His heavy footsteps echoed in the chamber as he approached Dragonfly.

"I am Commander Ariel Carter, of planet Earth, commander of Bug Team Alpha. My genetic line is none of your business," Dragonfly replied as she matched his advance step for step.

They met in the middle of the chamber like two gladiators ready for battle. Malrex glared at Dragonfly, but she did not look away. She did not back down.

One of the clones spoke up. "The Alpha Challenge has been declared and accepted," the male with red skin said. He held up a staff, as if to signal the start of the challenge. "This is a fight to the death. Are both combatants ready?"

"No!" Dragonfly declared. "Before we fight, I want some answers."

Malrex scoffed. "You seek to delay your fate," he said.

"No. I seek answers," the commander insisted. "I want to know why this ship is headed towards Earth. And how do I convince you to stop it?"

"Your planet has been targeted," Malrex said impatiently. "It will be harvested of its resources and stripped down to bare rock. Any survivors will become cyborg servants to the World Ship."

Dragonfly could barely hide her anger. Her hand tightened into a fist. "Why?" she asked.

"It is the way of the World Ship, and has been for countless generations," Malrex replied proudly. "I have harvested a hundred worlds as Alpha!"

"Why not just find an uninhabited planet to settle on?" Dragonfly suggested. "There are plenty of them in the Earth Colonial Coalition. You don't need to harvest other planets. We could help you find a world suited to your needs."

The court of clones began whispering to each other. It was as if they had never thought of this idea.

"Stop this ship! Let the Coalition help you," the commander shouted above the clones' murmuring.

"No more talk!" Malrex roared. The court of clones immediately fell silent.

"Just one more question," Dragonfly said. "What do I get when I win this challenge?"

"*If* you win, you shall become the Alpha of the World Ship," the red male with the staff said, as if it was obvious.

"OK," the commander said. Then she launched into the air.

The battle for the World Ship had begun.

CHAPTER 10

Commander Dragonfly lifted off the ground. She had hoped to catch her opponent off guard. But Malrex surprised her with his speed.

The Alpha leaped upwards on powerful legs and grabbed Dragonfly's ankles. The commander buzzed her wings and tried to lift Malrex towards the ceiling. But he pulled her down and slammed her onto the stone floor.

Dragonfly's armour took most of the blow, but she still got the breath knocked out of her. The commander rolled away just as Malrex stomped at where her head had been. The smooth stone cracked under Malrex's heel. Dragonfly took to the air again.

The commander swooped down at Malrex and fired her blaster. But Malrex had quick reflexes. He dodged the blaster fire and ran towards the display cases lining the walls of the chamber.

The Bug Team Alpha members shouted a warning, but Dragonfly saw what Malrex was up to. He was heading for an alien weapon in one of the cases.

Malrex smashed the case with his fist and grabbed a large lance from the display. The tip crackled with energy. He pointed it at Dragonfly and fired.

ZAAABOOM! A bolt leaped towards the commander.

But Commander Dragonfly had quick reflexes too. She twisted away from the bolt. It hit the ceiling. Gems fell like giant hail. The court of clones ran under an overhang along the side of the chamber. The clone escort fled into the corridor. Bug Team Alpha stood their ground.

A chunk of falling stone hit the commander. Her blaster tumbled from her hands as she faltered in midair. Dragonfly dropped to the chamber floor.

The Alpha sprang towards her. Before Dragonfly could get up, Malrex swung the lance. It caught the commander in the chest, knocking her back to the floor.

Again Dragonfly tried to stand. And again, Malrex swatted her down.

Dragonfly slid across the smooth floor. Although her armour offered some protection, her rib cage throbbed. Dragonfly gritted her teeth as she struggled to her knees.

Malrex chuckled as he walked over. Dragonfly lifted her head and boldly met the Alpha's gaze.

Malrex grinned. He took aim with the lance. Its tip crackled with energy bolts. "I am going to squash you, little insect," he hissed.

"Yeah, I've heard that one before," Commander Dragonfly replied. "I didn't listen then either."

She suddenly leaped at Malrex and grabbed the lance. Dragonfly ignored her pain. She was trained to fight through worse than a few broken ribs. The combatants fought hand-to-hand for control of the alien weapon.

Dragonfly swiped at Malrex's legs and knees, trying to trip him. Malrex held his ground. He slammed his chest into the commander and thrust his sharp horns at her head to frighten her. Dragonfly was not frightened. She tightened her grip on the lance.

Using the strength of her DNA-enhanced legs, the commander leaped into the air. She buzzed her dragonfly wings and flew to the peak of the ceiling.

Dragonfly did not let go of the energy lance. Neither did Malrex. Both hovered high above the chamber.

"I can drop you. You'll splat like a bug," Dragonfly warned. "Surrender, and I'll spare your life."

"I will die as Alpha!" Malrex hissed.

"No one can hear you up here. No one will know you surrendered," Dragonfly said. "I'm giving you an honourable way out."

"I will die as Alpha!" Malrex shouted.

Dragonfly looked into his angry eyes. She did not see any hope of convincing him.

"Then you will die," the commander declared, and she let go of the energy lance.

Malrex dropped. The Alpha fired the lance wildly as he fell towards the chamber floor. Dragonfly easily dodged the blasts.

Malrex landed with a thud. The alien lance tumbled from his hands.

But despite the fall, Malrex wasn't finished. He was struggling to get to his feet. Dragonfly landed lightly next to him. Before he could make another move, she wrapped her arm around his neck in a choke hold.

The Alpha thrashed and kicked with a final burst of energy. But Dragonfly's hold did not weaken.

"Yield, and I will spare your life," Dragonfly whispered, giving him one more chance.

"I will die as Alpha," Malrex wheezed.

"If you insist," the commander said. "Scorpion!"

Scorpion walked solemnly towards Dragonfly and the enemy. She knelt next to Malrex and looked at the commander. Dragonfly nodded.

Without hesitation, Scorpion plunged her spikes into Malrex's neck. His body went limp.

"The Alpha is dead! I have won the challenge!" Commander Dragonfly declared.

The clone court walked over to examine Malrex's body. Then they turned and bowed to Dragonfly.

"Long live the Alpha," they said with one voice.

Dragonfly winked at Scorpion. "Keep an eye on him," she whispered.

Then Dragonfly approached the throne. As she sat down, she recognized what the throne really was. It was a command chair that controlled the mega-ship.

"Bug Team Alpha! Attend me!" Dragonfly ordered.

The team stepped up to the throne and gathered around their Alpha.

"Help me figure out these controls," Commander Dragonfly whispered.

Aboard the Colonial Armed Forces flagship *Ares*, General Barrett received an unexpected comm transmission. It was from the mega-ship. But it had a familiar voice.

"Commander Dragonfly!" Barrett said. He did not even try to hide the relief in his voice.

"Hello, sir," Dragonfly replied. "Bug Team Alpha is in control of the mega-ship. Engines have been stopped. Forward progress is stopped."

The *Ares* bridge crew broke out into cheers. Barrett did not try to quiet them. "Excellent work," Barrett said over the noise. "It's not an overstatement to say that Bug Team Alpha just saved Earth."

"Thank you, sir," Commander Dragonfly replied simply. "I have a question, sir."

"What is it?" Barrett said.

"Not to be flippant, sir, but where do you want me to park this thing?" Dragonfly asked.

EPILOGUE

Three Earth Standard days later, Commander Dragonfly flew the mega-ship towards a lush, uninhabited planet on the edge of Earth Colonial Coalition territory. As the new Alpha of the World Ship, she was the only one whom the clones permitted in the command chair.

But Bug Team Alpha travelled with her. So did a group of Coalition advisers, relocation experts and medical teams. The *Resolve* flew as escort. Later, it would return the Bug Team and Coalition personnel back to Earth.

Radar and Locust stepped up to Dragonfly in the command chair. "We found the ship's historical records," Radar reported. She handed the commander a compact visual device loaded with the info. "It's a fascinating read. This ship has been in space for generations."

"And has it always been populated by clones?" Dragonfly asked.

"No. But the original inhabitants couldn't keep up the population numbers needed to run the World Ship," Locust replied. "They started cloning people to fill it. That became the norm over time. The natural descendants eventually died out."

"Then an elite group of clones calling themselves the Ancestors took control," Radar added. "Not long after that, the Ebon clan seized power and became a line of Alphas. That's when the World Ship started harvesting the resources of whole planets to supply the vessel."

"Since then, the clone population has only been produced from the DNA of the twelve Ancestors – the clone court," Locust explained. "The tans sort and store harvested materials. Reds are in charge of the engine assembly, and so on. Each clone type has a specific job."

"And what about the hive-mind behaviour we saw?" Dragonfly asked.

"It's a way to keep the worker clones under control," Radar replied. "As soon as they reach a certain age, microscopic nano-bots are injected into their brains."

"Can they be removed? I don't want to leave these people open to that kind of mind control ever again," Dragonfly said.

"I don't know about removal, but you could erase the nano-bots' programming," Locust said.

"Actually, you can do anything you want on the World Ship," Radar added. "You're the Alpha now. This ship and all of its people are yours to command."

"No pressure," Dragonfly said, rolling her eyes. She pressed a touch pad on the command chair. It activated the communication grid monitors all over the ship. "Attention, citizens of World Ship. This is the Alpha speaking. I am initiating new orders."

"Upon arrival on your new world, you will elect a new Alpha. He or she will guide you for a term of five local planetary years. Then you will elect a replacement Alpha. This will continue into the future. Genetic separation is hereby abolished. Nano-bot injections are abolished. Cloning is abolished. From this point on, everyone on this ship shall be considered an individual. Further announcements will be made later."

Dragonfly ended the transmission and turned to Radar and Locust. She grinned. "How do you like those commands?"

A little while later, Commander Dragonfly toured a factory inside the World Ship. It had once been used to transform the populations of harvested worlds into cyborgs. Now the facility was a hospital dedicated to reversing that process. The people were being restored.

As Dragonfly walked through the corridors, she saw many unfamiliar alien species. These people had come from planets far outside Coalition territory. But the teams of Coalition surgeons were doing their best to remove the cyborg implants. When the people were healed, they could choose to go home. Or, they could stay. Everyone was invited to live on the new world.

The only individual who was not invited was the former Alpha, Malrex. He sat in the brig aboard the *Resolve*. Scorpion's venom had not killed him. It had only knocked him unconscious. The clones had not known the difference and had officially declared Dragonfly as the new Alpha. Now Malrex awaited his sentence – detention on a prison planet.

After Commander Dragonfly had settled the World Ship into orbit above its new home, she was free to leave the mega-ship. She and the rest of Bug Team Alpha went aboard the *Resolve*. Their mission was complete. But Dragonfly wanted one last word with the former Alpha.

Malrex sat up and growled at the sight of the commander. Dragonfly ignored his greeting and pulled out a compact visual device. She played a video of the people of the mega-ship arriving on the surface of their new planet.

"Finding a new home was the original mission of the World Ship. That is, until your ancestor took over and declared himself Alpha," Dragonfly told Malrex. "We found the historical files."

"I am proud of my ancestors. Their genetic line was uninterrupted," Malrex declared. "I was cloned and raised to be Alpha. But you, Dragonfly, you are a genetic nightmare. You're not an Alpha – you're a bug."

"Actually, I'm both," Commander Dragonfly replied proudly. "Which makes me certain you'll never forget Bug Team Alpha."

TOP SECRET AND CONFIDENTIAL

**TO: GENERAL JAMES CLAUDIUS BARRETT,
COMMANDER OF COLONIAL ARMED FORCES**

**FROM: COMMANDER ARIEL "DRAGONFLY" CARTER,
BUG TEAM ALPHA**

SUBJECT: AFTER ACTION REPORT

MISSION DETAILS:
   Mission Planet: Artificial alien mega-ship
   Mission Parameters: Prevent mega-ship from
      Earth impact
   Mission Team: Bug Team Alpha [BTA]
   * Commander Ariel "Dragonfly" Carter
   * Lt Gustav "Burrow" Von Braun
   * Lt Sancho "Locust" Castillo
   * Lt Irene "Impact" Mallory
   * Lt Akiko "Radar" Murasaki
   * Lt Madhuri "Scorpion" Singh

MISSION SUMMARY:
   Colonial Armed Forces ship *Resolve* dispatched to
destroy asteroid on collision course with Earth. BTA
Lt Burrow on board to test prototype space armour on
asteroid surface before destruction. Test revealed surface
to be the hull of an alien mega-ship. Ship did not respond
to communication attempts. BTA dispatched to enter
vessel and stop impact with Earth.
   Interior of mega-ship discovered to be a Dyson
sphere – an inverted environment. BTA encountered and
destroyed automated defence robots. Living population
discovered on board. Contact revealed the humanoid

inhabitants to be clones under the influence of a hive mind. Direct communication was ineffective. BTA independently learned location of the primary engine assembly. Due to unexpected ship acceleration, BTA travelled to assembly to gain control of the vessel.

Engine shutdown achieved without resistance. BTA was in process of locating navigation controls when attacked by cyborg security squads. Cyborgs were neutralized. A message was unknowingly delivered through cyborgs' mechanical implants – a challenge to be Alpha, leader of the mega-ship.

BTA was escorted to a central command cube. There, BTA encountered twelve master models for the ship's clone population. Only the Alpha was unique. Alpha revealed the mega-ship was travelling to Earth to strip it of its resources.

The Alpha challenge was non-negotiable. Commander Dragonfly, being the "Alpha" of Bug Team Alpha, was forced to engage. The commander won the challenge. Dragonfly took control of the ship and stopped its course towards Earth.

Mega-ship was piloted to an uninhabited planet suitable for the ship's population to colonize. Former Alpha was transported to Prison Planet 5.

APPENDIX 1: EQUIPMENT REQUISITION
"Burrow" prototype space armour
BTA customized space suits
Zip-Class transport ship *Arion*

APPENDIX 2: PARTICIPANTS
Bug Team Alpha [mission participants listed above]
Captain Addo, Colonial Armed Forces ship *Resolve*
Research and Development Tech Team [prototype armour]

END REPORT

Glossary

alloy material made by melting and mixing two or more metals, or metals and nonmetals

assembly group of machine parts that make up one unit

collision act of two or more things violently running into each other

exoskeleton hard structure on the outside of the body that gives support or provides protection

genetic relating to the physical traits or conditions passed down from parents to children

humanoid being that looks similar to a human

juggernaut large, powerful force or object that cannot be stopped

propulsion force or power that makes something move forward

protocol code of correct behaviour usually seen in diplomatic or military services

recon search for information about the enemy; *recon* is short for *reconnaissance*

relic object that is from a past time

About the author

Laurie S. Sutton has been interested in science fiction ever since she first saw the *Sputnik* satellite speed across the night sky as a very young child. By the age of twelve, she was reading books by classic sci-fi authors Robert Heinlein, Isaac Asimov and Arthur C. Clarke. And then she discovered *STAR TREK*.

Laurie's love of outer space has led her to write *STAR TREK* comics for DC Comics, Malibu Comics and Marvel Comics. From her home in Florida, USA, she has watched many Space Shuttle launches blaze a trail though the sky. Now she watches the night sky as the International Space Station sails overhead instead of *Sputnik*.

About the illustrator

Patricio Clarey was born in Argentina and studied Fine Arts, specializing in illustration and graphic design. After graduating he moved to Barcelona, Spain, where he's worked as a conceptual artist, book cover illustrator and art director of a magazine. He also illustrates graphic novels and is the artist and coauthor of *Archeologists of Shadows*. Patricio's work has been featured in several publications, including Ballistic Publishing's *Exposé 9* and *Exposé 11*, which showcase some of the best digital art from around the world.

Discussion questions

1. *Juggernaut* is an example of a book in the science fiction genre. Discuss which details in the story make it science fiction. Have you read other books or seen films in this genre? Do they have anything in common with *Juggernaut*?

2. As the leader of Bug Team Alpha, Commander Dragonfly sometimes has to make tough decisions. For example, she ordered the team to move out while the alien boy was still stuck in the pit. Talk about a time when you had to make a tough decision. How did you feel afterwards?

3. In Chapter 7, the story switches between the action on the asteroid ship and the action aboard the *Resolve*. Why do you think the author chose to go back and forth between the two settings? How did it make you feel as you were reading?

Writing prompts

1. Write a summary of what you think will happen to the World Ship inhabitants as they settle on their new home planet. If you're up for a bigger challenge, write a chapter from the perspective of one of the clones or former cyborgs. Use descriptive words to make your story come alive.

2. Bug Team Alpha faced many dangers aboard the World Ship. List the different combatants. Which one do you think is the most dangerous? Explain your answer using examples from the story.

3. The Colonial Armed Forces need your help! They need a report on Malrex, the former World Ship Alpha, for their records. Be sure to include a physical description, a description of his personality and any other details you think are important. Look back in the story to make sure your report is accurate.

BUG TEAM ALPHA

THE DIG

LAURIE S. SUTTON

When an archaeologist goes missing, Bug Team Alpha is called in to investigate. But there's more to this mystery than meets the eye...

STRANDED

LAURIE S. SUTTON

Bug Team Alpha's transport ship has crash-landed after entering an interplanetary war zone. Can they survive and rescue themselves?

INVISIBLE ENEMY

LAURIE S. SUTTON

Talos is under attack, but no one can see exactly who - or what - the enemy is. Only Bug Team Alpha is equipped to handle the fight.

THE TIME VORTEX

LAURIE S. SUTTON

A time machine has trapped half of Bug Team Alpha in 1600s Japan. Can they find their way back home, without changing history forever?